THOMAS & FRIENDS

Thomas and Scruff

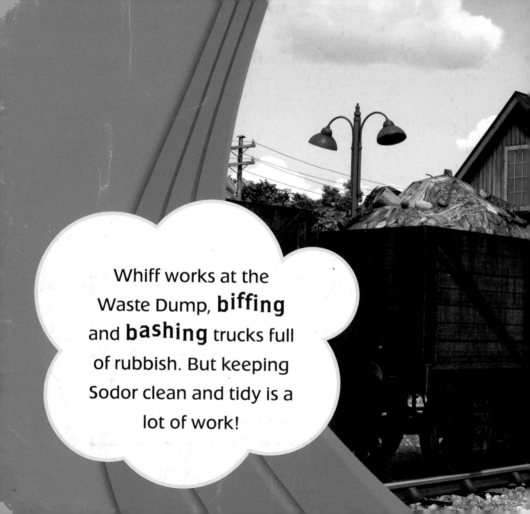

Whiff works at the Waste Dump, **biffing** and **bashing** trucks full of rubbish. But keeping Sodor clean and tidy is a lot of work!

One day, Thomas had good news for Whiff.

"I'm fetching a **helper** for you today," he peeped.

Whiff was **very excited!**

Thomas met Scruff the Scruncher at the Docks.

"Hello," Scruff chuffed. "I can't wait to **scrunch** some rubbish!"

Thomas liked Scruff, but he thought he looked very **dirty**.

An idea flew into Thomas' funnel. He asked Scruff to wait for a special surprise.

Then Thomas chuffed away to gather some **brushes** and **buckets**, and **soap** and **sponges**.

Back at the Docks, Thomas showed Scruff his surprise.

"With a **splosh** and a **splash**, you'll be **clean** in a **dash**!" he peeped.

But Scruff was **scared**. He had never seen soap or brushes before!

With a **clickety-clack**, Scruff **whooshed** away and hid in a siding.

Thomas saw that Scruff was scared of being clean. "Please come out, Scruff!" he puffed.

But Scruff wouldn't come out.

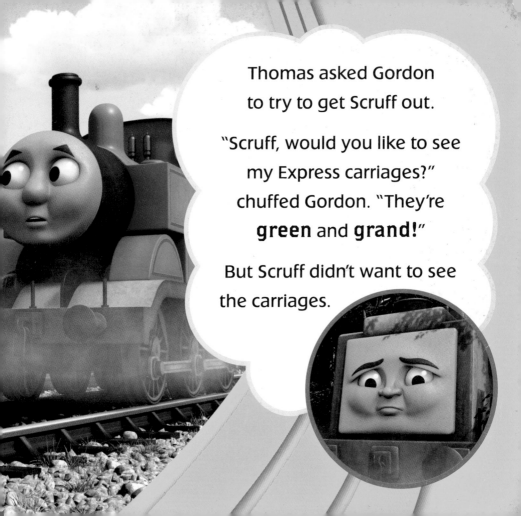

Thomas asked Gordon
to try to get Scruff out.

"Scruff, would you like to see
my Express carriages?"
chuffed Gordon. "They're
green and **grand!**"

But Scruff didn't want to see
the carriages.

Next, Thomas asked Henry to try.

"Scruff, would you like to help fetch my special coal? It makes me **fast** and **fearless!**" huffed Henry.

But Scruff didn't want to fetch the coal.

Then, Thomas asked Percy to try.

"Scruff, would you like to pull my mail trucks? They're **packed** with **parcels!**" peeped Percy.

But Scruff didn't want to pull the mail trucks.

Finally, Thomas remembered the one thing that Scruff **wanted** to do.

"Scruff, would you like to **scrunch** some rubbish at the Waste Dump?" puffed Thomas. "You don't have to be clean for that."

Scruff **wheeshed** out of the siding. He was ready to go!

Thomas and Scruff steamed to the Waste Dump, where Whiff was waiting. Scruff looked around the **dirty** dump.

"I'm going to like it here. There isn't any **soap!**" he whistled. And everyone laughed!

PEEP! PEEP!

The End